LOVING MYTHBUSTERS

CONNOR WHITELEY

DEDICATION

Thank you to all my readers without you I couldn't do what I love.

CHAPTER 1
2nd October 2023
Canterbury, England

University student Lewis Ward sat on a large brown fabric armchair in his brand-new student house that he had moved in with his friends yesterday. He had to admit that he had been nervous as hell because he hadn't known what to expect, and it wasn't exactly like his friends were well-known for their great tastes.

The house could have been a bombsite and they all would have loved it.

But Lewis was glad that the house was large, airy and really modern. Something that not a lot of students got to enjoy without it costing them thousands of pounds in rent each month, something Lewis was more than grateful he didn't have to put up with him, as the house was owned by his best friend Eddie's dad.

The living room was rather large with bright blue

walls that reminded Lewis of the ocean on a rare cool summer day, with thick, perfectly soft blue carpet that Lewis had been surprised at yesterday. It always made him feel like he was walking on a pillow, and the large paintings of ships, wrecks and divers hanging on the walls were impressive as hell.

He had no idea at all why Eddie's dad hadn't moved the paintings out the second he learnt a bunch of university students were going to be living here, but the house was great. Lewis was glad Eddie wanted him to live with him and their other friends that they made last year when they all shared a kitchen together on campus.

Lewis looked up at the sterile white ceiling as he heard banging, tapping and moans as he could have sworn Eddie didn't have anyone round last night, but he had gone to bed earlier after finishing moving in so Eddie could have had ten men over for all he knew.

The wonderful smells of bacon, sausages and eggs whiffed in from the kitchen as their friends Thomas and Ellis were making breakfast for everyone. Then they were going to go for their lectures and Lewis couldn't deny that made a cute couple.

Lewis smiled to himself as he couldn't believe that he was living in a house filled with gay men. A few years ago that would have been impossible, and Lewis was fairly sure that even if he was *allowed* to do it or given the choice, he would have said no.

He just didn't want to expose himself to

something he had been conditioned for over a decade to believe was wrong, but now he was out, happy and living with a lot of brilliant friends.

It was a massive shame they were hot as hell but in relationships, hook-ups or kindly not into Lewis. He didn't mind. Lewis liked them for being friends a lot more than anything romantic but it would be nice to have his first-ever boyfriend at some point.

But he couldn't deny that he felt guilty about wanting a man. It was a small silly feeling in the pit of his stomach, but at times whenever he looked at another man he would just feel guilty for wanting him.

It was stupid and he was glad he was unlearning what a decade of homophobia from his parents and family had done to him, but he still knew it was there. Just waiting to expose itself whenever he was vulnerable.

And he just knew that whatever man was brave enough to love him would ultimately leave in the end, because they couldn't handle him and his pain and his past.

He wouldn't blame them at all.

Something he really hoped today would help with.

"There you go sugar," Thomas said bringing him a plate of sausages, eggs and bacon with a good serving of mayonnaise. "I don't know how you can have mayo on everything,"

Lewis smiled. "It's nice and I am not a traditional

sort of man,"

"Amen to that," Ellis said as he bought in his own breakfast and sat on one of the large black sofas next to Thomas.

"So what work are you doing today?" Thomas asked.

Lewis grinned as he absolutely loved being a student ambassador for Kent University, where he got to go into schools and talk about how great, inspiring and fun higher education could be. And this work opportunity today had to be his favourite job yet.

"It's called a Mythbuster Programme where we go into schools and talk to students about what it's like to be LGBT+ and a university student," Lewis said grinning.

"Now that would have been great to have at my old school," Ellis said. "Could you imagine how many months of pain and suffering we could have been spared from if someone told us at that age, that we were okay and there was nothing wrong with us?"

"Exactly," Lewis said, "and that is really what I love about it. Not only does it give me and others from our community the chance to bust myths about university and being gay. But we get to talk to students and tell them that they're okay. And not deranged or whatever rubbish they're heard,"

"You might be the hero of our house," Eddie said as he came into the room in only his boxers.

Lewis knew he stared for just a moment too long

but Eddie had a great body with abs, biceps and a very large wayward part. And Lewis was determined to get himself a boyfriend sooner rather than later.

He had to explore that side of being gay and free and really happy with who he was.

"Is this the first Mythbuster session sugar?" Thomas asked.

Lewis nodded as he ate a lump of sausage. He loved the sweet juicy flavour of sage, apple and succulent meat as he chewed.

"Do you know anyone else going today?" Eddie asked.

"No," Lewis said, "I know there's three of us but I don't know anyone. I might have seen them across the room last year during training but I hadn't really had a chance to talk to them,"

"I know Fianna's going," Ellis said. "She's an excellent Lesbian who really knows how to talk about her life, her loves and everything in a very inspiring way,"

Thomas playfully kicked his boyfriend's ankle. "You almost sound jealous of her girlfriend,"

"No of course not," Ellis said, "because I doubt she can do what you did to me last night,"

Lewis just smiled because it was *this* reason that was why he loved living with other gay people. They could talk, just be gay and just have normal sex conversations that straight people would have turned their noses up at them for doing. This was what he wanted, needed more of.

And Lewis just didn't know exactly how much of this he was going to get.

CHAPTER 2
2nd October 2023

Canterbury, England

Alex Cole pulled his tight-fitting black overcoat tightly around himself as he sat on a brown wooden bench just outside Kent University's main reception area. The massive grey, metal building wasn't exactly the most ugly building in the world but considering Kent University had some beautiful buildings made from glass, different coloured metals and even more interestingly textured concrete ones, the reception building had to rank the lowest for Alex.

He was meant to be meeting Ashley, a great woman from the university that was chairing the session today, so she could give him a lift to the school.

She wouldn't turn up for a few more moments, which wasn't the best but it could have been worse, as an icy cold wind brushed Alex's cheeks. He would have loved to be in the warm, cosy inside of the reception area but he didn't want Ashley not to be able to see him.

A few black and red and blue cars slowly drove down the long main road just outside the reception area, with plenty of staff cars lining the road. Alex nodded as a large group of male and female students in their large coats came out of the huge yellow-bricked accommodation block opposite him and went off towards their first lectures of the day.

Alex had always liked the Kent University campus a lot more than he probably should have. It was so big, had everything he needed and everyone was just so friendly. Something he was really glad about considering what his secondary school had been like.

Alex noticed a slight scent of lilacs, jasmine and coffee fill the air as a very tall woman in a bright pink coat came up to him. This had to be Fianna, and Alex couldn't deny that her brown skin looked great against the vibrancy of the pink coat.

"Are you Alex?" she asked.

"Yes and you must be Fianna," Alex said extending his hand.

"Are you nervous?" she asked.

Alex smiled, because it was only now that he was realising that he was. He had never spoken about his gay experiences before to strangers. He was really looking forward to it but he was a little nervous too.

His hands were a little wet, his stomach churned and tightened and his throat was as dry as a desert.

Alex had always known that kids and older students could be horrible when they wanted to be, but ultimately he knew that they were fine. And they didn't care but it was still useful to give them a chance to ask questions, find out more about university and the best benefit was that Alex got paid.

"I take that as a yes," Fianna said. "I am too but we'll be fine,"

Alex just hoped that she was right as Ashley came now. He had worked with her a couple of times and it always ended with him smiling, laughing and being completely stress free. Out of everyone from the Outreach department that Alex had had the pleasure to work with, Ashley had to be his favourite time and time again.

She was brilliant but Alex wasn't sure she was actually going to make it to her car as she struggled to walk wearing her black boots with three-inch heels.

"You okay there?" Alex asked.

"Maybe," Ashley said smiling. "My husband bought these for me to make me taller. I don't think he knows how tough these are to walk in,"

"My girlfriend did the same," Fianna said. "It was a nightmare to walk in them and I just binned them when she wasn't looking,"

"I might do just that," Ashley said.

Alex smiled. He was really glad that this was Ashley's project for the university, and it was extra nice that because her child was right in the middle of transitioning from female to male, Alex was glad to have that extra perspective.

The perspective of a straight person with a trans son.

All perspectives were just as good as each other.

Ashley gestured they should start going towards her little black car that was at the end of the road. Alex stayed close to her just in case she fell and he needed to save her.

Alex was never going to let anything happen to an innocent person.

"Just saying," Ashley said, "I have never done this before and I don't know too much about your own experiences so everything will be fine, but I am flat out nervous about this,"

Alex laughed. Normally he relied on Ashley for making everything so easy, so stress-free and for making things work so smoothly that he didn't notice if anyone was nervous of not.

Clearly that wasn't happening today but Alex didn't mind at all. He was going to be with great people and he was finally going to get to be himself in public, talking about things he cared about and he was going to bust some myths about the community he loved.

Little did Alex realise he was about to discover something else to love too.

CHAPTER 3
2nd October 2023

Canterbury, England

"Thank you for signing in, just take a seat please,"

Lewis thanked the school receptionist as he sat down on a very spongey purple fabric chair without any arms as he waited in the school reception area waiting for Ashley and the other two ambassadors to turn up.

He had never been to this particular school before but he really liked it. The reception area wasn't really much of anything more than a hallway with large glass doors separating the school with the reception area.

He could see all the boys and girls sitting on long plastic benches having their breaktime catch-up, games and talking about how evil school was. Lewis guessed there easily had to be a thousand schoolchildren out and about in the dining area and around behind the reception desk where he heard more voices.

A couple boys and girls looked at him like he was a strange alien that was too young to be there for official business but too old to be a student. So the students looked at him for a few more moments and then went back to their conversations.

Lewis had no idea what at all what they were talking about. All their deafening voices merged into one super voice that cancelled out each other to just create noise.

And there was a hell of a lot of it.

Lewis noticed there were three long lines of schoolchildren preparing to buy themselves a cookie, a bacon roll or something else he couldn't identify from the row of silver serving platters at the very end of the dining area. Lewis never liked school meals, they were always made with the poorest ingredients and it wasn't hard to tell.

It was just good to see the schoolchildren here were happy, calm and talking non-stop with their friends. Lewis really hoped that calmness would continue into their little talk.

Lewis held his stomach slightly as he felt it churn again. He had no idea why he was so nervous, he spoke with Ellis, Eddie and Thomas constantly about gay stuff and debating how wrong the myths about gay people were. He didn't know why he was so nervous about this?

Maybe it was something to do with his parents

but Lewis didn't mind. He forced the thoughts away and he was looking forward to meeting the students because Ellis had definitely been right earlier about wanting this at his own school.

Lewis wasn't sure how much of a difference this would have made, considering the issues at home, but even if a single person, a single teacher, student or ambassador from a university had come into his classroom and told him that he was okay. And having these feelings towards someone of the same sex were okay, then Lewis truly knew those words would have been lifechanging.

That was exactly what he wanted to achieve today.

Someone fell into the glass door from the reception side.

Lewis jumped as he noticed Ashley had fallen off her three-inch heeled boots and she was looking angry as anything.

"Give from the husband?" Lewis asked grinning.

"You have no idea Lewis. I am done with these boots and I would even sell them to a child, I'm that angry,"

"Doesn't that go against safeguarding procedures?" Lewis asked smiling because Ashley was a fully-trained safeguarding officer.

Ashley stood up, took a deep breath and smiled. "It is good to see you again Lewis, the other two are just coming because they're parking,"

"You allowed two university students to park

your car for you?" Lewis asked knowing that Ashley really had no boundaries with ambassadors at times.

Ashley shrugged and went over to sign herself into the school and to help the nice lady on reception to summon their school contact for them, so they could all be taken to the classroom where the children were going to meet them.

"Where did you learn how to park like that?" a woman, probably Fianna, asked.

Lewis looked at the two people coming into the reception area. Lewis nodded at Fianna who he had heard a lot about and it was going to be interesting hearing her talk and then he looked at- holy fuck, fuck, fuck.

Lewis just froze. He went light-headed. His stomach churned. And he could feel the drops of sweat pouring off him as the reception area felt like an oven.

Lewis had flat out never ever seen such a fucking gorgeous man in all his life. He loved how fit, skinny and sexy the man was in his tight-fitting blue ambassador t-shirt they all had to wear. And the man's black slightly ripped jeans with the knees open showed Lewis the gorgeous man didn't have any leg hair.

The man was smooth, cute and his face was to die for.

Lewis's thoughts ran a thousand miles per hour trying to take all of the man's stunning beauty in just in case he wasn't going to get another chance.

Then as the hot man stopped in front of him. Lewis just focused on his pointy, cute, amazing face with his shiny, soft, lustrous brown hair parted to the left in a much more attractive version of the bowl hairstyle.

This man was divine and now Lewis had to go into a classroom, talk about gay experiences sitting next to the most beautiful man he had ever seen.

That was going to be a very pleasurable and long session.

CHAPTER 4
2nd October 2023

Canterbury, England

As Alex walked closely next to Ashley to make sure she didn't fall over yet again, as they went along the long dirty white corridor trying to dodge schoolchildren like no tomorrow. He flat out couldn't believe the extremely hot, sexy god walking next to him.

Alex had never ever even remotely seen longish blond hair that looked so soft, velvety and perfect. He wanted, needed to run his fingers through that soft stylish pillow of hair and he so badly wanted to kiss Lewis's soft thin lips.

Alex couldn't believe how tall and fit Lewis was. It was clear as day he didn't have any muscles or anything too exciting under his ambassador t-shirt but Alex didn't care. He was fit as fuck.

Alex kept looking at him every moment he got and occasionally sexy Lewis would catch up and Alex would force himself to look at Ashley instead of the divine sex god next to him. It was even worse that he was finding Lewis really attracted at an LGBT+ university event.

It was either really poor taste that he was finding a man hot or if there was such a thing as the universe or whatever other nonsense people called, this just seemed like a cruel twist of fate.

Especially as he couldn't even talk to Lewis because they were working and there wasn't even enough time for a quick briefing.

Alex followed Ashley and the school contact, a very fit male PE teacher in his early twenties with a very typical gym body, into a large classroom with the walls covered in maths posters and little sayings to help the students.

There were rows upon rows of blue hard plastic chairs that every single school Alex had ever been to used for the fun of it, and it dawned on him just how many students could be coming. It would be brilliant if there was a massive turn-up for some reason he just doubted that any students would want to turn up to this little event.

Especially as the school had changed it all of a sudden from a compulsory thing to something else.

Alex didn't want to say in front of the teacher how much he flat out hated that. The entire idea behind these "little" events (as the PE teacher had called it) was to make sure that straight people were exposed to queer people so they got to meet them, see them and learn that they weren't stereotypes.

Clearly the schools had other ideas about apparently forcing their innocent students to see real queer people. It was stupid but Alex knew over time that would hopefully change as word about their Mythbuster event spread through the teacher grapevine it was what normally happened with very positive results.

"How do you guys normally do this?" the school contact asked.

Ashley looked at them all. "I was thinking how about we grab three chairs upfront and then we do it like a panel,"

"Like we're important," Alex said, instantly hating his silly words but he was glad when Lewis smiled.

Alex, Lewis and Fianna grabbed three chairs from the back, and Alex really liked watching Lewis move so wonderfully, gracefully and he was just beautiful in the way he walked. Alex really wanted to hear his story.

After they had all put their chairs down at the front and sat down, the teacher offered them tea and coffee where Alex and Lewis were the only ones to take a milky coffee.

Alex thanked the PE teacher as he took the coffee and enjoyed the warmth pulsing through him. It was a great contrast to the icy coldness outside, but he couldn't understand the loud roaring sound outside.

Until he realised it was a massive sea of students coming towards their room.

Alex smiled at Lewis and Fianna. He couldn't deny that Lewis had the cutest, pearly white grin he had ever seen and Alex never wanted him to stop smiling. And as Alex's stomach filled with butterflies, he wanted to swear about how Lewis made him feel great but schoolchildren were coming in.

Alex was pleased it was 16-year-old students in sixth form as it was these students that were starting to think about university in a year's time. And whilst Alex didn't doubt most of these students already had some idea if they were straight or not, he was still looking forward to doing a lot of good for them.

He just really, really hoped that their questions were going to be at least innocent or not completely immature. He would die if someone asked him an embarrassing sex question.

Thankfully they were more than able to say no to answering something.

A few moments later after Ashley had introduced the session, given out little yellow sticky notes so the students could write down questions as they went, Alex smiled at Lewis as he could see how excited he was.

He didn't really care how Fianna was feeling at the moment but Lewis was just so captivating and alluring and Alex really wanted to sit next to him but Fianna was in the way.

Then after Alex said his name, sexuality and

introduced his subject at university and the others did the same, Ashley asked the first introductory question.

"When did you first realise you weren't straight?" Ashley asked. "And let's start with you Alex,"

"It was about in year 8 so about when I was 13 and I had just moved up a class, and there was this blond boy. Really sporty and attractive and that's how overtime I realised I was getting more and more interested in him, before I realised that my feelings of attraction were different to my straight friends. And that's how I started my journey towards understanding that I was gay,"

Alex loved questions like that because it was always a question that needed rewording towards straight people, because he had always been different, always known he was gay and he had realised that he was different to other people. But all the straight people in the room where expecting an answer about him "coming out" to himself.

Something no gay person really did, so he did have to sort of play up to some expectations of the audience.

Then after they were listening, he could start to bust some myths and Alex was looking forward to hearing Lewis's answer a lot more than he ever wanted to admit.

CHAPTER 5

2nd October 2023

Canterbury, England

As Lewis listened to Fianna give her answer to the first introductory question, he really liked looking at all the male and female students in their black school uniforms, because he could always tell a lot about them and how any school event was going to go just by looking at their reactions.

The blue plastic chair was way too hard for Lewis and he was so glad that once he left secondary school he didn't have to sit on the awful things again. They were just so uncomfortable and he felt sorry for all the students that had to spend six hours a day on these silly chairs.

Lewis liked how there were about twenty students in here, slightly more girls than boys, but some looked interested, some looked expressionless and some looked like they were only here to get out of a lesson.

Yet he wouldn't lie, he was a little concerned about a group of sporty-looking boys in the back of the classroom. They were grinning and giggling and muttering to each other.

He doubted they were going to cause any trouble because no school ever allowed that to happen, but he was interested in the sort of questions they might ask. Especially as one of them, a tall ginger boy, was writing questions like no tomorrow on Alex's response.

Lewis felt his stomach churn and fill with butterflies as he pretended to focus on Fianna but he was really looking at beautiful Alex. He looked so cute, sweet and attractive as he nodded along and smiled to Fianna.

Lewis wasn't listening at all to Fianna but it was great how supportive Alex was towards other people. And Lewis got the sense that Alex was a really great guy, even more so with how he was walking next to Ashley earlier to make sure she didn't fall over. Lewis had only been walking next to her to film her falling over.

And make sure he didn't laugh too loudly, knowing Ashley would have done the same to him.

"And it was meeting my girlfriend that made me realise I wasn't straight," Fianna said.

Lewis nodded as he felt like he was meant to right now and then he realised he had to reveal how he had known he wasn't straight.

"So looking back I had always felt like I was different to other people and I had always had some attraction to boys. But it was only when I was 14 years old in PE after school practice one night that I realised I was gay,"

Lewis noticed Alex grinning like a little schoolboy himself. He was so cute.

"Because I was on the football team at school and we were all changing one night, and my friends started talking about girls and I just didn't react. I couldn't see the appeal so I mentioned it,"

Fianna gasped.

"Relax," Lewis said, "it didn't go badly. Yet after that everyone expected I was gay and I started myself exploring what being gay was and everything that gay people normally do to start exploring their sexuality, but my parents were not supportive at all when they found out,"

Lewis noticed that Alex was really cute as his face was a beautiful mixture of concern, attraction and wanting to hug him. Something Lewis really wouldn't have minded.

Lewis looked back at the students and he was really pleased to see one of the sporty boys and two of the other boys in the room really focusing on him. He really hoped his story about being sporty and not having accepting parents would help them.

If it had then the mythbusting session would have worked perfectly.

"Okay thank you," Ashley said, "and for our next introductory question how have your friends and family reacted to you not being straight?"

"My parents didn't care and neither did my

friends and family," Alex said. "Because, I think my fellow ambassador can back me up here, no one at university actually cares that you're gay. It isn't seen as weird, odd or anything else,"

"Exactly," Lewis said. "And even though my parents and wider family weren't accepting at all. University has been great for me because I have found that student community that just doesn't care about me being gay,"

Lewis liked seeing some of the students' faces light up at that announcement.

"And I would say," Lewis said, "that if you live in an unaccepting social world then I want you to know it can get a lot better. Tons better over time. It might take years but it does get better,"

As Fianna started talking, Lewis was surprised to see Alex just grinning at him and Lewis realised it was a good idea to have Fianna sitting in-between them because it was harder for others to tell that they were looking at each other so much.

And a wash of emotion washed over Lewis because it was great talking about this stuff, talking about being gay in a positive, friendly light and seeing that it was helping the students too.

"Thank you ambassadors," Ashley said flicking through a bunch of notes she had gotten out of a bag Lewis hadn't noticed she had come in with. "And our final introductory question because we're already covered some of them, is what myth would you like to bust today?"

Lewis leant forward. "That there isn't a set type of person that is gay. A nerd can be gay. A footballer can be gay. A perfectly straight-acting man can be gay. The whole idea that gay men are all girly is complete nonsense so that is what I want to bust today,"

Alex nodded. "Exactly and I want to bust the myth that all gay men are only interested in sex and hook-ups,"

Lewis grinned as he noticed Ashley trying not to laugh because this was not the direction where any of them wanted this session to go in. But in all fairness this was a Q&A session with a bunch of 16-year-old boys and girls.

This topic was always going to come up.

"Just like straight people, gay men and women are interested in relationships too with feelings, love and everything else that straight people experience too,"

And Lewis could have sworn Alex had said all of that just for his benefit. But what were the chances of that?

CHAPTER 6

2nd October 2023

Canterbury, England

Alex was seriously loving the session an hour later as the students had asked the teacher if they could stay just a few minutes longer to finish up the questions and close the session. He was so grateful that the teacher had said yes.

Alex had been really pleased with the questions that some of the students had been asking. There were always going to be some uncomfortable sex questions from 16 year olds but Alex, alluring Lewis and Fianna had avoided them or simply gave a vague answer.

But it was the questions from the sporty boys at the back that had really surprised him. It was definitely nice, from what Alex had worked out, that one of the students was gay and it was him and his friends coming here, so the gay student could find out more. And his straight friends could support him.

Alex was fairly sure it was the getting out of class that had made the straight friends want to come along, but it was brilliant how they had still wanted to come here, support their friend and get involved. Alex supposed they could have asked nasty questions or just stayed silent but they were actually some of the most active students.

Granted Alex wished someone would open a window because it was starting to smell of flowery perfume, teenage boys and sweat a little too much for Alex's liking but he felt so relieved the session had gone so well.

"And for the final question to close the session with, I'm coming back to my notes with *what would you tell your 16-year-old self?*" Ashley asked.

Alex flat out loved this question because it had to be such a powerful note to end the session on, and he was looking forward to seeing what beautiful Lewis was going to say.

"That even if you are lonely at school," Alex said, "because you don't have many friends and many gay friends. At university or the wider world you can find your crowd that will love, support and help you to embrace whoever you want to be,"

Alex enjoyed seeing a whole bunch of students looking at each other and nodding like that was sort of lifechanging information that they needed to chew on a little more.

"Don't listen to the haters," Fianna said. "You are perfect just the way you are,"

Alex completely agreed. He had never heard truer words.

"I would say," Lewis said, "just remember no matter how dark and how bad it seems. It does get better. It might take months, years or more years than you want to admit but it does get better and you can be happy,"

Alex smiled at Lewis to make sure he felt he was supported here of all places, but he couldn't help but wonder what his life story was. His answers were always on the darker, slightly more negative side but Alex didn't get the sense that he was a negative person.

If anything from watching him for the past hour, Lewis used his negative past to empower himself and Alex knew that was incredible, and definitely something he wanted to find out more about.

Alex smiled because he wanted to explore so much about Lewis, and most importantly if he had a boyfriend or not.

A few minutes later, all the different students were smiling, thanking them and leaving so Alex and Lewis put the chairs back and the teacher thanked them for their time as he closed down his laptop. Alex was sure the teacher had been using the session to catch up on paperwork which he didn't mind at all.

Teachers didn't have enough time in the day as far as he was concerned.

Then the teacher led them all back down the long dirty white corridor filled with boys and girls of all different ages running up and down trying to get to their lessons.

"How did everyone find that?" Ashley asked turning slightly as she walked.

Alex went closer to her to make sure she didn't fall over. "Great thanks, the students seemed really into it and positive,"

"Actually," the teacher said, "the students in the session have really found this useful. They're all not exactly straight but no one has the vocab to talk about this sort of stuff with them and there is a lot of us teachers who aren't able to help them,"

Alex knew it was a risky question because he was still technically working and by extension he was still representing Kent University.

"What do you mean?" Alex asked looking at Ashley in case he had crossed a line.

"The headteacher knows she's going to have twenty thousand phone calls tonight from parents angry about us exposing students to queer people," the PE teacher said holding open a door.

Alex started following them down a long metal spiral staircase that he guessed was only used by staff members.

"But being exposed to gay people doesn't make a person gay," Lewis said.

The PE teacher laughed. "I know that, my boyfriend knows that, everyone knows that except some parents,"

Alex was really surprised the PE teacher was gay

and almost kicked himself for thinking just because he was a PE teacher with a stereotypical gym body he couldn't be gay.

And as the teacher dropped a folder he was carrying under his laptop and bent down to get it, Alex had to admit knowing he was gay definitely made him more attractive but nowhere near as attractive as Lewis.

A few minutes later, Alex got his black overcoat out of the boot of Ashley's car and wrapped it tightly around him as the icy coldness of the early October afternoon wrapped around him. The car park was quiet with no one else about as Ashley dived in the car with Fianna as she had made sure they were all okay and had given them a little debriefing.

Including the little bit of information about there was another Mythbusting session booked two weeks Friday.

Alex was really looking forward to that.

He saw that Lewis was about to walk away so Alex gently placed a hand on Lewis's wonderfully warm, smooth arm.

"Did you want to grab dinner, coffee or whatever at some point?" Alex asked completely failing to hide how nervous he was.

Lewis grinned like a schoolboy and grabbed a pen and scratch of paper from his pocket. "This is my number, call me and I'd like to see you again,"

Alex just stood there completely frozen as he watched Lewis walk back to his own car so beautifully, elegantly and perfectly like he was a divine stunning angel walking amongst them.

Maybe Lewis was, he was attractive enough and Alex really wanted to get home and call Lewis and he just hoped he didn't have to wait too long for their date.

Something he was a lot more excited about than he had any right to feel.

CHAPTER 7
6th October 2023
Canterbury, England

After spending the past few days texting, calling and video chatting with beautiful Alex, Lewis flat out couldn't believe how excited he was for tonight. They were going to a little restaurant in the heart of Canterbury, he was going to get to know this amazing man and Lewis just wanted everything to go perfectly.

It probably would because he couldn't see how anything could go wrong when he was next to someone so beautiful, but Lewis still wanted to be careful.

Especially as he just knew that Alex would leave him in the end when he learnt who Lewis really was.

Lewis sat on his favourite armchair in his living room right next to a brand-new shipwreck painting that Eddie's dad had wanted the men to look after. Lewis didn't know if Eddie's dad was crazy or something for giving university students something so important, precious and beautiful to look after but he didn't mind.

There was no one else in the living room yet and Lewis liked that. It meant he could scroll through Alex's social media in peace without being interrogated. It was a shame that Alex didn't post anything even remotely revealing or sexy, but the more he looked at his rare posts (from what Lewis could tell Alex posted three times a year), the more Lewis realised he didn't need anything revealing. Alex was just sexy the way he was.

Lewis heard Ellis and Thomas come in through the front door after returning from their lecture, and Lewis supposed he really did need to do the assigned reading before his own lecture in a few hours. But he was so excited for tonight that he didn't want to.

"Afternoon sugar," Thomas said as he came in, went into the kitchen and popped the kettle on.

Lewis looked up at the ceiling as he heard Eddie finish with one of his latest hook-ups and Lewis was surprised he didn't get excited about the idea of Eddie coming downstairs in his boxers again. Something that was way too common for his liking at times.

"How was the lecture?" Lewis asked.

"You know," Ellis said coming in, "there's only so many ways you can do advanced mathematical equations,"

Lewis just nodded. He never really cared about Ellis and Thomas doing their maths degree. It went way over his head and he really didn't see the point in it, but Lewis was man enough to admit he was only saying that because of his ignorance.

"Afternoon lads," Eddie said coming into the living room with only his shirt off for a change.

And Lewis looked for a moment but actually didn't care about Eddie and his chest. Sure Eddie had a six-pack, large biceps and a perfect body but he really didn't care.

He had no idea why. Maybe it was because of Alex but Lewis didn't know that was possible. They had only been texting and calling and videochatting for a few days. Surely he couldn't have blocked off all other romantic options in that short a time.

Eddie stood right in front of Lewis. "What's wrong?"

Lewis looked over to Thomas and Ellis who also looked shocked.

"Mate," Eddie said knelt down on the ground so he was eye level with Lewis. "What's wrong? Whenever I come in here topless or less you get excited,"

"I do not," Lewis said failing to hide the fact he was lying so badly.

"Am I ugly now or something?" Eddie asked.

"No, you really aren't. I just don't think I'm interested anymore," Lewis said really not wanting to admit he had a date tonight.

"He's met someone," Ellis said.

"Really sugar?" Thomas asked getting all excited.

Lewis laughed and stood up but not before

gently placing a hand on Eddie's large shoulder by *accident*. They really did feel as hard as they looked.

"Yes, tonight I'm going on a date with a beautiful guy I met on Monday," Lewis said enjoying how his stomach filled with butterflies at the very idea of spending a whole evening with Alex.

"I know that look," Ellis said hugging Thomas. "That's the look Tom gives me,"

Lewis grinned. He was so looking forward to tonight and he was really glad that his friends were supporting him instead of interrogating him.

He never would have had that level of support at home.

"Where are you going sugar?"

Lewis shook his head. "No way in hell am I going to tell you that, because I know you two would want to spy,"

"Why wouldn't I want to spy?" Eddie asked.

"Because it's a Friday night. You will be too busy pounding your way through the rest of the Canterbury student population," Lewis said laughing.

Eddie blushed and Lewis hugged him, and he was surprised when Eddie moved closer to his ear.

"Do you want any tips about sex for tonight?" Eddie asked.

Lewis shook his head. "It's one date and I'm not the type of gay to have random sex so instantly after just meeting a guy,"

"You've known the guy for four days," Eddie said. "Normally I've had sex with them ten times during that time,"

"Let the boy date his own way," Ellis said.

And as the rest of the conversation turned towards sex, dating and past horror stories about dates gone wrong, Lewis just grinned through all of it. He had never heard, met or even been allowed to have these sort of conversations before.

And they were great to hear, laugh at and gasp about because they made him a lot more excited for tonight.

So excited that he was pretty sure he was going to explode way before tonight.

CHAPTER 8
6th October 2023
Canterbury, England

Alex really liked that he might have been a second year at university but he was still allowed to stay in university accommodation. It might have been more expensive than non-campus accommodation (barely) but at least he got to meet first-years and he got to be on campus where all the action was.

He was alone in his little university flat that he was still getting a little used to. His flat last year had been large with bright white walls, a very high-end single bed that he basically had to jump up on and his desk took up one half of the longest wall.

This flat was a little different.

It was a lot smaller with him barely being able to swing a cat in the flat. Alex wasn't a massive fan of his bed because it was so low it was basically on the floor so he always tripped over it coming back from a lecture. And even worse the walls were bright orange.

He was at a university not the Caribbean.

Alex tried to focus as he went over to his small brown wardrobe and he pulled out a few different options for tonight. He wasn't sure if he wanted to go smart, casual or sexy.

Those were his three main options.

Someone knocked on the door, and as much as Alex just wanted to crack on, he opened it.

"Hi there sweetie," a woman called Eva Marshall said.

Alex waved her in because they had spent a lot of great nights in their shared kitchen talking, laughing and debating various topics as both of them did environmental science.

She wore a thin little blue skirt, white blouse and looked like she was heading to a business meeting instead of preparing for whatever Friday night plans she had.

"You going somewhere?" Eva asked sitting on his bed.

"Yeah I have a date with a really cute boy. He's an ambassador like me and we're going to the *Diamond's Heart*, you know that little place in Canterbury where all the couples go,"

Eva laughed. "Sweetie that place is perfect and my boyfriend took me there once. It was a wonderful evening, you will love it but I do have one question,"

Alex looked down at his three clothing options. He certainly didn't want to wear a suit so he wasn't going with the smart option. He gestured her to continue.

"Is he very experienced?" Eva asked.

Alex laughed because he just couldn't understand why everyone thought all gays were just sex animals that only did kissing, sex and hook-ups. Not every single gay man was into that, exactly how not all straight people were into relationships and starting a family.

"I doubt it but this is a first date," Alex said. "I have no intention of doing anything more than kissing him at the most,"

Just at the idea of kissing Lewis' soft, perfect, sexy lips made Alex grin and his stomach fill with butterflies. He really, really wanted to kiss him.

"Okay, okay I was only asking because believe me sweetie, the last thing you ever want is to look forward to sex only to find that the man is awful at it,"

"That's a little harsh for your boyfriend," Alex said smiling.

Eva playfully kicked him and Alex laughed because Eva's boyfriend had turned up twice to their shared kitchen, and Alex had an excellent sense that he was great in the bedroom.

Alex held up a pair of blue jeans, a perfectly ironed white shirt and some black shoes. It wasn't exactly formal because he wasn't wearing the trousers (not that he did that matter anyway) but it was still a little too much. Or was it?

Eva stood up and folded her arms. "What's

wrong? Let me help you sweetie?"

Alex showed her the shirt and jean combo which she didn't look too excited about, so he went back to his clothing options and grabbed a slightly more textured and colourful blue shirt.

"That might work better," Eva said.

Alex picked out a thin cream-coloured jacket and Eva gave him a thumbs-up.

"That would be perfect, but you really like this boy don't you sweetie?" Eva asked.

Alex wasn't sure for a moment why she would ask. Yet he couldn't deny that the last days of calling, texting and just waiting with a stomach full of excitement had been wonderful. Lewis just made him feel so light, young (which he was) and positive that he realised he did like Lewis a lot more than he wanted to admit.

And as he looked at the time, he quickly threw Eva out of his flat, got changed and he raced towards the restaurant because he really didn't want to be late to the most important date of his life.

Because he knew, he truly true that this could be *the* date with the *one*.

CHAPTER 9
6th October 2023

Canterbury, England

Lewis was seriously impressed with the Diamond's Heart just off cobblestoned Canterbury High Street. He sat opposite the most beautiful man in the world and he couldn't deny that Alex looked sensational in his blue jeans, wonderfully fitting blue shirt and black shoes that really did highlight his fit body.

Lewis forced himself not to focus on Alex too much just in case he couldn't control his wayward parts that really wanted to spring free of his own jeans.

He was still really impressed that Alex wanted to see him properly, guys never normally wanted to do that with him. Yet Lewis truly knew that it wouldn't last because Alex would leave him as soon as he learnt how messed up he was.

Lewis really liked the gentle orange warmth of

the place that gave it such a cosy, warm and exotic feeling. There were plenty of small little round tables where cute young couples (and some older couples) sat around smiling, giggling and flirting with each other.

There was a straight couple to his left and Lewis knew the woman in her little black dress was in for a great night ahead, because it was clear the young man in his suit was head over heels for her. And that was lovely to see and really heart-warming.

Lewis had to admit the lighting wasn't brilliant for seeing the prices on the menu, that for some reason were in a different coloured ink than the menu items. Yet the lightning really did make him feel nice, romantic and like he really wanted to have sex with Alex immediately.

He shook the thought away because he just wasn't sure if that was what *he* wanted, or if it was just a decade of sexual suppression wanted to explode out of him.

Alex was so cute.

"I never did find out what you were studying," Alex said, "and I know, before you ask, you said it on Monday but I was focusing too much on you instead of your words,"

Lewis grinned. Alex was so sweet and he couldn't judge Alex at all. He knew there were plenty of things Alex had him that Lewis hadn't listened to at all.

"I do psychology specialising in forensic psychology and no before you ask, it isn't profiling.

Profiling is a rubbish thing designed by the FBI and it isn't based on science at all. Psychology is,"

Alex grinned. "How many times have you had to dispel that myth?"

Lewis couldn't believe the first real thing he had ever said to such a cute man was him almost moaning. He had to get better at learning when someone was attacking him and when it was just in his own head.

The consequences of his childhood never failed to amaze him.

"I'm sorry. A lot of times and I just get tired of it all. I guess it's why I like the Mythbuster programme so much because I get to counter myths and get paid at the same time," Lewis said picking up the menu.

"Definitely, and the getting paid bit is always nice too," Alex said smiling. "What we doing starters, mains or all three?"

Lewis just focused on how adorable Alex's smile was for a moment before realising he actually wanted an answer from him.

"Why don't, we stretch this out as long as possible and go for all three?" Lewis asked.

Alex laughed. "I'll try but I have a small stomach,"

"Probably why you're so fit," Lewis said out of instinct.

Alex laughed and Lewis was so glad he didn't find that too much too soon. Lewis couldn't understand why he was saying random things to Alex, he never normally did. Whenever he spoke to anyone he liked to think of himself as careful and considerate.

Then there was Alex who was making him say all sorts of things without an ounce of thought. It was so annoying.

"You're fit yourself and I like your body," Alex said knowing he was making Lewis flush. "If you don't mind me asking though, what were the circumstances of you coming out?"

Lewis frowned a little but smiled as a waitress came over, they ordered drinks and sadly beautiful Alex asked the same question again.

Lewis really didn't want to talk about it and he had a feeling that Alex would have been perfectly okay if he didn't tell him. But Alex was so kind, cute and Lewis had already mentioned it in public in front of a group of school kids so not telling Alex felt like he was kicking him in the mouth.

And Lewis never wanted to do that to such a sexy man.

"To say that my parents weren't supportive was an understatement and they just don't like gays. I don't think they're religious but if there's a myth about gays then they believe it truly. It doesn't matter how dark, how twisted or extreme the myth they believe it,"

Alex nodded and Lewis was surprised. When he first told Ellis, Thomas and Eddie about his past, they had instantly reacted, supported him and more. Lewis was surprised at how nice it felt having Alex just want to listen to him before reacting.

"Their favourite myth was that gay people were wild sex machines that couldn't control themselves around other men and boys. And when my parents were out in public and they noticed a gay person, they would immediately grab me and my siblings and make sure we didn't see the gay person,"

"But surely having such a strong reaction only made you notice them more. And I take it they believed the rubbish about being exposed to gay people makes you gay,"

Lewis nodded. It was nice to just talk about the myths and how messed up his family was.

"No yes and ever since I came out to them last year they hadn't spoken much to me. They said they want to pay for my accommodation and stuff but that's the extent of their involvement in my life. I don't really want to talk to them and they don't want me to see the rest of the family,"

"In case you turn the rest of your family gay?"

Lewis laughed. "When you say it in that tone it sounds stupid,"

"That's because it is and your family are stupid for not wanting someone as passionate, nice and beautiful as you in their life,"

Lewis smiled as the waitress returned with their drinks and admired Alex as he elegantly drank his diet coke like he was an angelic or some other divine creation.

He really was that irresistible but Lewis was going

to try and stretch out this date for as long as possible just so he didn't have to stop looking at someone as stunning as Alex.

CHAPTER 10
6th October 2023
Canterbury, England

A few hours later, Alex was seriously pleased with how stunning, juicy and flat out incredible the steak was, the chips were so peppery and crispy and the peppercorn sauce was simply to die for. He had loved talking to Lewis about everything and nothing and the evening had been amazing.

Alex smiled as he watched stunning Lewis finish off his pie and chips and Alex felt so lucky to spend tonight with him in such a great restaurant. Granted Alex wasn't really a fan of the bright orange walls because they reminded him way too much of his flat.

Yet everything else about it was perfect.

Alex wrapped his hand around his ice cold glass of diet coke and he was glad that Lewis felt comfortable enough around him to talk about his past, his parents and everything he had been through.

Alex had heard plenty of negative stories, met

plenty of men over the years who had had poor family support and he was glad his parents were so great towards him. He felt sorry for Lewis but he was so cute as he just ate away at his pie.

And as much as Alex didn't want to mention it to Lewis, but he wouldn't have been surprised if Lewis would have a lot of issues to overcome as their relationship went forward.

Alex forced himself not to react as he wasn't sure they were in a relationship, it was their first date and as great as it was, he didn't want to hurry it along. If Lewis had the type of childhood he had heard about then he needed to make sure that Lewis was comfortable, happy and he was learning that being gay was perfectly okay.

And he needed to know all of those things at a deep level.

"That was great," Lewis said putting his fork down, "but you never told me why you said you didn't have many friends at school?"

Alex smiled. He should have known this was going to come up sooner or later because he had mentioned it to the schoolkids.

"I wish I could give you some great story about it but truth was, I wasn't popular at school. I was brainy and everyone liked me a lot because I was a *cool kid* and really nice. Just no one wanted to be my friend,"

He was expecting Lewis to judge him or something but he didn't. Beautiful Lewis just sat there, listening and Alex was fairly sure he was going to make sure Alex was done before he shared his ideas.

Alex didn't know how to take it. Normally whenever he said he wasn't popular at school, someone always jumped in saying that they were foolish for not wanting him and that things had changed now and all the rest of the rubbish people said to be nice.

But all Alex truly wanted was someone to listen to him.

"I guess it was partly my fault because I didn't really know what to do, I didn't know how to invite people out for things and people just didn't really ask me," Alex said.

"How are things now?"

Alex smiled. "Better, a lot better. I'm part of a ton of societies at the uni and I have a lot of friends on my course,"

"I'm glad because the world needs more people like you in it,"

Alex cocked his head. "Like what?"

"Kind, respectful and you are perfect company,"

Alex felt it wasn't an insult but he just wasn't sure it was the most flattening thing anyone had ever said to him considering they had spent the past two hours together.

Lewis laughed. "I'm joking. I've had a great night and you're a great, really easy, person to talk to,"

Alex nodded. "You aren't so bad yourself. What you doing next week?"

"You want another date?" Lewis asked sounding way too excited.

Alex laughed because he was barely managing to contain his own excitement. There was nothing more he would have liked than spending more time with Lewis.

"Yeah and maybe we can do something a little more active," Alex said.

"Sex?"

Alex shook his head. "No no no. I meant, I don't know we're thinking of something to do on our date. But thanks for tonight, it's been fun,"

As Alex watched Lewis wave over the waitress for the bill, a wave of sadness washed over him as they weren't going to see each other for at least another entire week.

Next week was busy as hell for Alex with lectures, assignments and seminars. He had no idea how he was going to last without seeing Lewis for a week but he was going to have to soldier on.

It wasn't exactly like he had much of a choice but he was just glad everyone had phones these days. At least that day he could text, phone and see Lewis's handsome face on a videocall.

That would definitely lessen some of the emotional pain of not seeing him but not by a lot.

Damn it. Alex couldn't believe how much he liked Lewis but he was feeling the best he had in a long, long time.

CHAPTER 11
13th October 2023
Canterbury, England

Lewis had to admit he was absolutely useless at planning a date, he had no idea why he had said to gorgeous Alex that he was going to plan a magical night and he had no idea why Alex hadn't stopped him. He had been trying all week trying to come up with something, anything that might show Alex how much he liked him, but he had failed.

Thankfully Ellis and Thomas had been around to help him come up with a semi-good night. Yet Lewis didn't like that the plan of a nice movie night and a home-cooked meal all depended on Eddie and his hook-ups *not* coming downstairs.

Something he knew was going to happen at least twice during the evening.

As Lewis stood with his hands on his hips staring at their large silver oven waiting for the timer to go off, he enjoyed the warm feeling of the hot steam washing over him and the entire kitchen smelt of tomato, garlic and chicken from the homemade chicken kiva that he was making.

The kitchen was large, modern and Lewis still thought that Eddie's dad was mad for giving a bunch of university students such a nice place that would be wrecked at one point or another.

As the doorbell went, Lewis froze as a weird sense of how wrong this date was washed over him. He couldn't help but think that it was wrong that he was inviting a man into his home, that he was cooking for a man and that he was going to spend an entire evening with a hot man that was probably going to end up in sex.

He pushed the thoughts away.

Lewis forced himself to focus on the here and now and he grounded himself by focusing on the sweet aromas of the chicken, garlic and tomatoes. His past was in the past and his parents were out of his life.

That was all that mattered.

The doorbell went again and again and Lewis went through the living room and opened it.

Lewis's mouth dropped as Alex stood there in his black jeans, black polo shirt and black trainers. Lewis had told him to be casual but he couldn't believe someone could look that great in only casual clothes.

Alex was to die for.

Lewis hugged him as he came through the door and as much as his thoughts about his parents slammed into his mind. He kissed Alex.

Alex gasped in surprise but Lewis loved the warmth, the feeling and the taste of Alex's soft divine lips.

It was the first time he had ever kissed a guy and Lewis wasn't disappointed. It might have been a quick little kiss but it felt so natural, so right and so perfect that Lewis wanted to do it again and again.

"You looked shocked?" Alex said. "Have you ever kissed a guy before?"

Lewis looked to the floor and shook his head. He shouldn't have done that, it was wrong and he would have waited until Alex was ready.

Lewis saw Alex was crouching down a little to make him look Alex in the eye and then Alex kissed him again.

This time it was soft, tender and a little messy but Lewis didn't care. He was actually kissing a man. This wasn't a fantasy, this wasn't something he did whilst wanking. He was actually kissing a real flesh and blood man.

And he loved it.

Lewis stood up straight and placed his hand on Alex's waist and he loved how fit, sexy and slim Alex felt against his hands. He was so looking forward to seeing how Alex's body felt against the rest of him.

Then the oven timer went off.

Lewis rolled his eyes and went off to the kitchen to sort out dinner and thankfully Alex followed him.

"It's very nice to see you," Alex said sounding a

bit surprised and pleased at their kissing.

"After that kiss I'm to see you too. I've never kissed a guy before so, I hope I wasn't too bad,"

Alex laughed. "Don't be silly you were great and you put effort in. A solid B+"

Lewis smiled and shook his head as he took the baking tray out of the oven. His stomach churned again as he was so looking forward to spending another great night with such an irresistible man.

He didn't care about anything else as he felt Alex come closer, so close that Lewis could feel Alex's body heat against him. He loved how close they were, he loved how Lewis wanted nothing want than to simply devour Alex right here and now and the sexual tension in the air was like a bomb about to go off.

Lewis looked at Alex who was just standing there. He wasn't doing anything, he wasn't trying to look sexy, he wasn't trying to do anything.

But after so many years of sexual suppression and fearing to be gay, Lewis just wanted to be with a man that could love him, respect him and show him how amazing being gay actually was.

Then he noticed the large ball of something pressing against Alex's jeans.

"You, um, wanna go upstairs?" Lewis asked.

Alex pretended not to be interested but Lewis could see his body really was.

"I don't want dinner to spoil," Alex said.

Lewis laughed and took Alex in his arms and they both laughed, kissed and started undressing each other as they tried to make it to the stairs.

But Alex tripped over and pulled Lewis down onto the thick, soft blue carpet that Lewis really liked all of a sudden.

"I guess we're fucking here then," Lewis said.

CHAPTER 12
13th October 2023

Canterbury, England

An hour later, Alex just laid next to an extremely hot, naked Lewis as the two of them laid next to each other and just hugged tightly after a great sex session. He had never done a virgin before and Alex was impressed it was as great as he imagined and Lewis wasn't anywhere near as bad as he thought he would be.

Alex focused on Lewis's hard body and chest as he rested his hand on Lewis's smooth chest as it rose and fell so evenly that it was almost hypnotic and calming enough to send him to sleep.

Alex felt so alive, calm and great that he was grateful that Lewis had given him the privilege of showing him the joys of gay sex and he had trusted him enough to allow Alex to have done what he did to him.

Alex watched as Lewis just stared up at the

ceiling. He hoped he wasn't panicked or anything because he knew that the first time could be scary. Especially when he had all the lies and myths and misconceptions floating about in his head that his parents had told him.

He just hoped Lewis would be okay and Alex really couldn't deny how attractive he was.

But the biggest thing that Alex was surprised about was how nice the house was. He really hadn't expected for Lewis to live in such a nice place like this, the living room was beautiful, the art was reasonably good and the carpet was so thick it was perfect for having sex on.

Alex heard people move upstairs and then he heard someone coming down.

Alex didn't feel the need to do anything because from what Lewis had told him it was probably only Eddie or one of his hookups, and Alex was really jealous that Lewis got to live in an all-gay house. He would have loved that.

The living room door opened and a very tall man with large biceps, a perfect chest and a massive boner in his boxers came into the living room and just went into the kitchen.

"I take it that's Eddie?" Alex asked.

"Yeah," Lewis said sitting up.

Eddie came back through the living room and grinned as the two of them laid naked on the living room floor.

"Good job mate," Eddie said to Lewis. "I'm

really pleased you finally managed to get some dick and you managed to land such a hot boy,"

Alex rolled his eyes as Eddie came over and knelt down on the floor next to him grinning, but Alex had to admit Eddie was enough of a gentleman to look mortified as his boner brushed against Alex's leg.

"Sorry about that," Eddie said kissing his hand. "You are hot,"

"He's mine," Lewis said laughing and shooing his friend away.

Alex nodded and Eddie shrugged as he raced back upstairs to continue his night with his latest hook-ups.

"We shouldn't have done this," Lewis said.

Alex rolled his eyes making sure Lewis couldn't see that.

"Eddie's right. You're hot, beautiful and you are an amazing guy but you don't deserve a guy like me with my past, my lack of experience and everything else,"

Alex shook his head. He couldn't believe this was happening.

"What do you mean?" Alex asked. "Who do I deserve then?"

"I don't know someone like Eddie. No, not him he's only interested in hook-ups. Someone definitely like Ellis and Thomas. They're a great couple and you really need a man that can give you the life you deserve,"

Alex stood up. He couldn't believe Lewis was

actually doing this straight after sex but Alex was determined to support Lewis no matter what.

"I know the first time is scary as hell and you *know*, truly know that you're gay now but it's okay. I was scared after my first time," Alex said knowing it was a massive lie.

"Really?"

"Yes," Alex said couching down and taking Lewis's hands in his. "If you just trust me then you'll know this is okay in the end. Nothing bad is going to happen and I don't want anyone else but you,"

He could see that Lewis didn't look sure.

"I don't want anyone else like Ellis and Thomas. I want you because you're cute, kind and you are an amazing person that needs to be happy,"

"You make me happy," Lewis said.

A wave of emotion washed over him and Alex kissed Lewis's smooth, soft lips. He really loved the taste of him.

"I know this is scary but together we're going to get through this okay. And you're going to learn that being gay is okay,"

Lewis nodded and Alex kissed him again but he could tell that the kiss was distant and nowhere near as passionate as it had been just a moment before.

He didn't know what was going on but he just wanted Lewis to be okay, happy and hopefully wanting to be with him.

CHAPTER 13
14th October 2023
Canterbury, England

Lewis had really loved having irresistible, sexy Alex slept next to him through the night in his own warm single bed after everything that had happened last night. He just stared up at the perfectly smooth ceiling of his bedroom brushing his fingers through Alex's hair as he rested his head on his chest.

He had no idea that gay sex could be that amazing, mind-blowing and just sensational before. It was so much fun and Lewis loved how he felt so light, alive and the greatest he had been for ages.

It was amazing that sex could do that to a person.

Lewis kept gently stroking Alex's hair as he felt that ugly feeling in the pit of his stomach rise up. He almost felt a little ashamed for actually having sex, his parents would have been gutted if they found out and they would probably stop supporting him completely.

He didn't want to lose them, he wanted to be allowed to see them and talk to them, and maybe sex was wrong and-

Lewis closed his eyes and forced himself to take deep breathes of the warm air that smelt so manly and wonderful of Alex, the man he treasured and really, really liked.

He was sure now that Alex would never leave him because he had been great last night. Lewis had been freaking out about sex and that ugly pit in his stomach had rose up right after sex. But Alex hadn't judged him, hated him or anything.

Alex had simply listened and Lewis couldn't believe how lucky he was that he got to sleep with such a hot man that wasn't just interested in sex, but he was kind, sensitive and great too.

Lewis's phone buzzed and he checked the email confirming that he was working at the Mythbuster event on Friday. He grinned to himself because it would be another great chance to talk to more schoolkids and show them that not all gays were girls, gay people weren't anything to be weirded out by and gay people were normal.

There weren't anything reasons to hate them, and hopefully he could inspire some other gay kids in the class that they were okay.

His phone buzzed again. It was from his mother.

Lewis opened it and he couldn't believe that the message read *I saw you out with a man the other day.*

He had no idea at all how the hell his mother had

found out. It should have been impossible.

Lewis had never even thought about his mother, father or any other member of the family seeing him and Alex out together. They had only been out once before and he hadn't noticed them.

Granted Lewis hadn't been focusing on anything but Alex because he was so damn beautiful. He had no clue what to text back to his mother or how to explain.

They had done nothing wrong at all.

"What's wrong?" Alex asked getting up and wiping the sleep away from his eyes.

Lewis showed him the text and judging by Alex's face there was another text that had just come through.

"I hope he isn't gay for your sake. You know I don't hate gays but I am hateful of the act," Alex said. "What does that even mean?"

Lewis couldn't believe this was happening so he covered his eyes with an arm. "It means that my mother or another member of my family saw us together at Diamond's Heart,"

"So? Why should we care? I really like you and I don't care what your family thinks," Alex said kissing his cheek.

Lewis laughed. Alex wouldn't get it because he was from a great home, a loving family and everything else that Lewis had never had.

Lewis hated it as his stomach churned again and again and he hated that sheer feeling of guilt rising up inside him. He could remember his mother's and father's sheer look of disappointment on their faces like it was yesterday and then hear the shouting between each other later that night when they thought he was asleep.

"You don't understand," Lewis said. "They will never accept you, us,"

Alex climbed over him and Lewis admired his fit sexy body. "I don't care what your parents think about us because I really like you and I want us to keep going with this relationship,"

Lewis grinned. He liked that too.

"Because we are boyfriends after all,"

"We aren't boyfriends," Lewis said out of instinct.

He hated how Alex jerked his body and Lewis couldn't understand why Alex was frowning and stiff and confused.

"What does that mean?" Alex asked.

Lewis shrugged. He had no idea what he had just said and why Alex seemed annoyed.

"I mean I really like you too," Lewis said. "You're amazing at sex, you're a great guy but we aren't boyfriends. We can never be boyfriends,"

Alex stood up and put his boxers on. "Why not?"

Lewis was about to reply then he realised he didn't have an answer. He searched his stomach and it was still churning but he couldn't tell if that whole boyfriend comment was him talking or his parents talking.

He really liked Alex. He was beautiful, hot and beyond amazing but Lewis was scared. He had never been in a relationship before and he couldn't see himself in one, not now or ever in the future.

And Alex was better off without him. Lewis knew he was an ugly wreck of a human that didn't deserve happiness, love or anything because his parents were right. He wasn't right and-

Lewis gasped as he realised exactly how badly he was fucked up.

"What's wrong?" Alex asked fully clothed and he knelt down and took Lewis's hands in his.

Lewis couldn't believe how much guilt, anger and confusion he had inside him. He was only realising now how much his parents impacted him, how many parts of him they had poisoned and how many thoughts they had put in his head that weren't his own.

He looked at beautiful, kind and caring Alex and Alex deserved better. And someone that was a lot less messed up.

"You don't deserve me. Just go and find someone that can give you everything you want," Lewis said hating himself.

Alex went to talk but Lewis just looked at him. He meant what he was saying because he was saving Alex from a lifetime of pain with him, because this wasn't a problem he was going to solve overnight or at all.

He simply didn't deserve love and Alex truly did.

"Call me when you're ready to have another go at this," Alex said, "but realise that you're the one leaving this relationship. Not me,"

Lewis blew him a kiss as Alex walked away and then his stomach relaxed perfectly.

"Damn you mum and dad. Damn you all," Lewis said as he collapsed onto the bed and just crawled up into the Fetal position and his eyes let it all go.

CHAPTER 14
14th October 2023
Canterbury, England

Alex had no idea what had just happened in Lewis's bedroom as he walked down the long dark road towards the nearest bus stop where he could hopefully get back to the university quickly.

The road was clear and wide and the bright white road markings were a weird contrast to the sheer darkness of the road and the black sky. Alex knew it was going to rain any minute, he just wanted to get to the bus stop first.

Alex liked the coolness of the air and how it smelt damp, fresh and had hints of freshly cut grass laced in it making the taste of late summer barbeques with his family form on his tongue. Those were a lot better days than today. Those were filled with laughter, happiness and love.

Not like today.

The icy cold howl of the wind blew past him as

he walked, and the quiet sound of cars swooshing past made for poor company. And Alex just hated all of it.

He had met more than enough gay men over the years to know, truly know what internalised homophobia was like, and how much damage the lies and constant hate from the people that were meant to love them could do to a person.

But in the end the person had to do something to help themselves.

His phone buzzed and he checked it. Alex grinned as it was a confirmation email saying that he was working on Friday at the next Mythbusting session in another school. He never liked how delayed his uni emails were at times.

He was so damn happy about that. He could talk to more students, make a difference in their lives and help them to learn that everything would be better in the future.

Something he hoped that Lewis would learn sooner or later.

Alex couldn't believe that he would see Lewis there again on Friday. He didn't want to see him. Lewis had hurt him too much for that but he forced himself to focus on the fact that he wasn't there for Lewis.

He was doing the Mythbusting session for all the young gay boys and girls that needed someone to support them, and to help the straight students understand a ton of truths about the LGBT+

community.

Alex nodded to a little old lady walking her small dog as they passed. And he wanted to go back to Lewis's house (mainly so he could shelter from the rain) so he could convince him that he had to change, get help and just do something more productive with his life.

Instead of simply allowing the hate to poison him, his life and his relationships.

Alex didn't blame him.

Lewis had to be one of the kindest, most caring and beautiful men Alex had ever seen in his entire life. Alex had loved kissing, hugging and making love to him because Lewis wasn't bad at it.

He really wasn't bad at being gay, bad at being himself or bad at anything. Lewis was always going to be the sweet, loving man that Alex was always going to love no matter what happened.

Or what obstacles were thrown up in their way.

A bang of thunder made Alex almost jump as the rain started pouring. Alex just frowned because he didn't have a coat, he didn't have an umbrella (not that any young person did these days) and he didn't even have a man in his life.

Alex saw the bus stop in the distance and he tried to quicken his pace but he was already soaked through. His shirt and jeans clung to him and he felt really fit but really unattractive at the same time.

He kept going towards the bus stop but he was half tempted to just stand there in the rain and allow the rain to wash him away. Or at least try to wash away his feelings.

Lewis had been such a hot man that had caught his heart, Alex never wanted to be away from Lewis, his lips and his gorgeous smile.

There had to be a way out to him, a way towards their relationship working or at least a way towards how there could be a future for both of them. He had no idea how that could happen but Alex was determined to find a way.

It didn't many how small of a chance a plan had of working, Alex was willing to take it because he believed in Lewis, he believed in their relationship and he certainly believed in their love.

He just had to find a way to make Lewis realise that. Something he didn't have a clue about how to do.

Not a clue at all.

CHAPTER 15

14th October 2023

Canterbury, England

"So you broke up with him to save him. That's dumb sugar," Thomas said.

Lewis just rolled his eyes and he hated himself utterly as he sat on the blue fabric sofa in their living room. He hated himself, he hated his life and he was so angry at what his parents had made him do to someone as beautiful, perfect and sexy as Alex.

The massive shipwreck painting on the wall in front of him looked exactly how Lewis felt, he just couldn't understand why he had done something so stupid. At the time he had truly believed he was saving Alex but now, now he knew he was just being a coward.

He was sabotaging his chance of happiness all because of family members he didn't even see anymore.

"I was a dick wasn't I?" Lewis asked.

Eddie sat down next to him and it was weird seeing Eddie clothed for a change. He looked good in his black tracksuit that highlighted his fit body but Lewis really wanted Alex.

Alex was the man he really liked, if not loved, not Eddie.

"Yes you were a complete and utter dickhead," Eddie said, "and we all understand *why* you did it but it was still wrong,"

"I managed to work that out for myself," Lewis said really wanting to text, call or videochat with Alex but he didn't know what to say.

Or even how to fix this?

Ellis pulled over an armchair. "You know I've done something like this before, not breakup with the love of my life but I know what it means to deal with internalised homophobia,"

Lewis didn't want to believe that. Ellis was such a rock, so confident, so good in the relationship department that Lewis had no idea how someone who felt such shame could possibly recover.

But he wanted to listen.

"I recover," Ellis said, "by talking about it to a therapist, talking about it with my friends and most importantly wanting to change,"

Lewis gulped at that idea. He had done some clinical psychology modules early in his degree and he remembered a lot of the mental health points about therapy. If a client didn't want to change then the therapy would fail.

It really was as simple as that most of the time.

"I want to change. I want to be happy, I want to be okay with my sexuality and I want relationships, but therapy? That's going to be a nightmare and with university I don't have time for that,"

"Then nothing will get better," Ellis said firmly.

Lewis didn't want his friends to be mad at him but it was the truth.

"And how would I get therapy? I don't have a severe enough mental health condition or something 'wrong' for me so I cannot get it for free on the NHS. I don't have the money to go private,"

"Get your parents to pay for it, sugar,"

Lewis shook his head. "Believe me that is definitely the last thing they would ever do for me,"

"If you truly wanted to change then you would find a way to get therapy, sugar. When there is a Will, there is a way," Thomas said so firmly that Lewis could have sworn he was almost being shouted at.

He wouldn't have blamed his friends at all if they wanted to.

He deserved it.

Lewis stood up and went over to the shipwreck painting hanging in front of him. He had never really paid much attention to the paintings before but he liked seeing how the black, dark blue and white brushstrokes swirled, twirled and whirled around each other even if the humans were screaming in the painting as they drowned.

"Why does your dad have so many paintings in

here?" Lewis asked. "He must know that a bunch of university students could easily wreck them,"

Eddie chuckled. "Seriously? You meet the love of your life at a Mythbusting event and here you are banging on about the same myths,"

Lewis smiled and laughed to himself. He was seeing this all wrong, this whole time he had been truly believing in the gay myths that his parents had been feeding him since birth, and even now when he claimed to be combating against them he was still allowing them to impact him.

He was believing in the lies that his parents told him about how wrong gays were, how gays were the devil's work and they didn't deserve happiness, and most importantly, the lies about gays were so fundamentally wrong they didn't deserve any kind of love.

They only deserved pain, hate and shame.

Lewis shook his head and focused on the tiny little humans on the grey sand beach and in the black water of the painting. Those people were drowning and Lewis didn't want to drown in the myths and lies and pain that he had allowed himself to be consumed by.

There was hope for a better future, there was hope for a better life and there was a lot of hope for a life with Alex. The man Lewis really loved.

He looked at his friends. "I need to figure out a way to get therapy and then I need to prove to the man I love that I can change for the better,"

Lewis loved as his stomach felt perfectly calm, happy and filled with butterflies at the idea of spending his life with the man he loved.

There was still work to do but Lewis felt like he was getting closer to where he could go back to the man he loved.

CHAPTER 16
17th October 2023
Canterbury, England

After three days of searching, contacting the university and a whole bunch of different NHS trusts, Lewis flat out couldn't believe how impossible it was for him to get any form of therapy. From the conversations he had had with a to bunch of mental health services, they really were stretched too thin to help him.

Lewis could understand that. He would have preferred the professionals to help those clients with crippling depression, anxiety and the most severe mental health conditions compared to him. In comparison those people who needed heart surgery whereas he only had a small cut on his finger.

They needed more help than Lewis.

Yet Lewis was surprised that the university's mental health support teams were very interested. When he had phoned them and visited them in person, they seemed to understand his difficulties and that he needed therapy, but they weren't equipped for it.

Lewis had to admit they weren't useless because they had offered him counselling but Lewis wanted, needed therapy. Since it wasn't the past that bothered him, it was his thoughts, his feelings and how he internalised all that hate and that could only be "cured" with therapy.

Something no one seemed interested in giving him at the moment.

"How's it going mate?" Eddie asked.

Lewis leant against the icy cold windowsill and looked out onto the long dark street as black cars drove past, schoolkids ran past with their parents chasing after them and even some dogs were excited and ran too.

Lewis had barely had the courage to look at the paintings today. He was trying so hard to get into therapy so he could improve, he could live a happier life and he could prove to Alex that he was a changed man.

It all seemed so pointless.

"Here you go mate," Eddie said passing Lewis a large mug of milky coffee.

Lewis liked the warmth that filled his hands and the great aromas of vanilla, bitter coffee and sweet creamy sugar as he noticed the foam on top. Sometimes he struggled and forgot that Eddie was a coffee barista and not just a hook-up obsessed friend.

"I hadn't heard anyone upstairs with you for a while," Lewis said smiling.

Eddie playfully elbowed him. "Maybe you got me thinking, you know. Maybe I am only doing hook-ups because I'm scared of something real,"

"What do you mean? I thought you've had boyfriends in the past,"

"Sort of," Eddie said taking a sip of his tea, "but I was really young back then and they were more boy toys than anything else. I've never had a 'real' relationship I suppose. I want one now though,"

Lewis took a small sip of his strong, bitter coffee that had just the right levels of sweetness, creaminess and the little shot of vanilla was amazing. Eddie was great at his job.

"What changed?" Lewis asked.

"My mum used to say something after she got divorced from my dad. She used to say *at some point Edward, you're going to learn you need to listen to when the music stops and just sit down,*"

"What the hell does that mean?"

Eddie laughed and almost spilled his drink. "I had no clue for the longest time but I think she meant that hook-ups and fucking every boy that moves is great,"

"Until you reach a point where you realise everyone else has relationships and you don't." Lewis said.

"Exactly mate," Eddie said. "I like seeing how cute Ellis and Thomas are, I like seeing you and Alex together and I want a boyfriend myself,"

Lewis sighed. "I'm glad you liked seeing us together because I'm sure that was the end of it. If I can't get into therapy then I know that I can't go back to Alex. Our fight or me being a dick will just happen again and again and that isn't fair on him,"

"You're a great boyfriend, you know?"

Lewis laughed and just took another great sip of his coffee. He supposed he could just take the counselling because it was better than nothing but he wanted something that would definitely work for the long-term.

Only therapy would do that for him.

And the only possible way that might work was for him to go private and pay the £2,000-plus that a full course of therapy would cost him.

Lewis grinned because he didn't have that sort of money but his parents did and because this was all his parents' fault. They might as well pay for it.

"I'm proud of you." Eddie said as Lewis took out his phone and dialled his parents.

As his mother answered the video call on the first ring, Lewis really hoped this was going to work because all his parents had ever responded to was strength considering they were bullies in their workplace too.

"Hi honey," his mother said. "I hope you got my text and I'll say again what I said-"

Lewis waved her silent. "Mum, you know I love you but you've fucked me up in more ways than you will ever know with yours and dad's hate, homophobia and all the lies you poisoned me with,"

His mum frowned.

"So," Lewis said, "I think we need to reset our relationship and I am going to give you two choices. The first one is we simply don't talk again, we forget about each other and we each live our own lives. I don't want that but I am prepared to do it,"

"This is because of those gay friends of yours. I told you they're influencing you, using you for your ass and all those other disgusting gay things *those* people do,"

"Or choice number two, you pay for me to get therapy so I can develop healthier relationships and unlearn so much of the crap you taught me. And that way we can start our relationship brand-new and I can still be your son,"

"Why would we pay for your gay brainwashing therapy? If you want conversion therapy we'll pay for that in a heartbeat,"

As much as Lewis wanted to only say yes to that option because it was more expensive than therapy, so he could pay for the therapy and still get some more money for himself. But he wanted to reset their relationship, he didn't want to lose his parents and right now it felt like that was the only choice.

"Mum," Lewis said, "when we hung up the phone today. If you chose option 1 then it will be the last time we talk and I will be happy not to talk to you again. But I want a mum and-"

"You're clearly high or something or being too influenced by those gay friends of yours. Call me when you're ready to be a real man again,"

Lewis ended the call and threw his phone across the room.

It smashed right next to the shipwreck painting that Lewis just shook his head as he went down on the floor and just grieved for what he had lost today.

They might have been toxic but he still loved his parents.

CHAPTER 17
18th October 2023
Canterbury, England

After meeting with friends, his fellow gays at the university's LGBT+ Society and talking to his parents a lot more than he ever wanted to admit over the past few days, Alex had finally come to the same conclusion as everyone else.

Unless Lewis wanted to help himself then there was nothing anyone could do for him.

He couldn't deny that he was impressed as hell about everything he had achieved, everything he had tried to discover about how to help a person like Lewis and how everyone had tried to help him. Because something that he was starting to discover now was that the LGBT+ community really was a community that wanted to love, support and make sure that everyone was okay.

When he had been talking to the LGBT+ society, he had spoken to people he had never ever been that bothered talking to, but as soon as they learnt that Lewis (a fellow member of their community) was in trouble they had wanted to help.

And Alex was damn proud to be part of a community like that.

Granted they hadn't got anywhere but that didn't matter because it was the thought that counted and Alex was really glad it had all worked out like that. He had made new friends, he wanted Lewis even more and he was more determined than ever to help Lewis.

The man he loved.

But as he kept walking along the long road up towards Lewis's house because Alex was just going to plead his case, make sure that Lewis knew they could solve all these problems together and that he loved him. Alex noticed that the road looked completely different today than only a few days ago.

Alex hadn't expected an October day to be so mild, not too cold and not too hot. He was half-tempted to take his jacket off but it looked cute so he kept it. The bright sunshine kept shining down on him and he just grinned.

He was finally going to talk to Lewis after everything that had happened.

The road was a lot quieter today without a single car going up or down it, and there wasn't even many parked cars outside the long row of semi-detached houses that lined the road.

Yet Alex really liked the sweet sound of children playing in the back gardens, laughing and screaming out in happiness about whatever young kids screamed about these days. Alex didn't really know but he didn't care.

A few moments later he got to Lewis's front door and he was surprised that he hesitated.

He took a long deep breath of the mild, damp air that smelt of lilacs, roses and lavender from the front garden next door. And he prepared himself to knock, he wanted to tell Lewis how he felt, that everything was going to be okay and he would support him no matter what.

But what if Lewis didn't want him?

Alex paused. He didn't want to get hurt again, he didn't want to suffer a lot of pain like last time, he didn't want to get rejected.

Rejection hurt a lot.

Alex knocked once.

After a few moments no one was coming to the door so Alex was about to turn around and leave, partly grateful that there was no chance that sexy Lewis could ever hurt him again.

"Hey," Lewis said as he opened the door.

Alex grinned as he looked at the beautiful man he had been missing for days. Even now Lewis was only in a tight-fitting sexy tracksuit but he looked divine. He had no idea a man could look that great in a tracksuit before now.

"I didn't think I would see you again after, you know," Lewis said.

"After you told me to forget about you and find

someone new, you mean?" Alex asked smiling.

He had missed Lewis so much, he had missed how great he was on the eyes, how beautiful his smile was and just everything about him.

"I'm glad you came," Lewis said, "because I wanted to tell you that I've been working really, really hard the past few days to show you how much I want to change and improve and be better,"

Alex took a few steps closer. He wanted to hear this because it proved that Lewis cared about him and wanted them to work. Exactly what Alex wanted too.

"Just ask Eddie and the others how many mental health services, charities and more in the past few days I've contacted because I want to deal with my past. I want to be better for you and I want to have healthier thoughts,"

Alex hugged him. "I believe you, I don't need to ask Eddie. Thank you for trying I appreciate it."

Alex loved it as Lewis hugged him back ten times harder and Alex coughed a little as he felt like his ribs were about to break.

"I did it because I love you Alex. When I saw you walk away and I realised my stupid mistake it almost killed me inside. There isn't another man on this planet that I would want. I want only you,"

Alex broke the hug and grinned. It was simple words and gestures and phrases like that, it was all he had ever wanted to hear from the beautiful lips of another man.

He had always wanted a kind, caring and sexy

man to say that he loved him and wanted to be with him. Because that was the thing about myths about gay people, they were everywhere and they were in every facet of life and society. Alex knew that his parents had been great and amazing and he loved them, but he still missed having a man in his life.

He supposed in a small way that even he believed that two men couldn't find happiness, love and a worthwhile relationship that would last long into the future.

But as Alex jumped up and he kissed and laughed with the man he loved, he knew that it was an utter myth and lie. Because gay people could be just as, if not more, happy than straight people because gay love was right, pure and amazing.

"I love you too," Alex said.

Alex was so grateful that Lewis had shown him that it was truly possible and not just something he said thinking it was true, because now he knew that it *was* true.

And that their love was going to last long, long into the future.

CHAPTER 18

20th October 2023

Dover, England

Lewis had flat out loved the past two amazing days having stunning, beautiful, funny Alex back in his life. They hadn't really left each other's side since they had got back together and now they were planning on slowly moving Alex into the house, or the Big Gay House as they were jokingly calling it.

Lewis didn't care what they called it as long as Alex was in it and they had talked, had plenty of sex and just loved spending time together. Lewis actually had no clue what life had been like before he had met Alex.

It certainly wasn't as good as these three weeks had been.

It was even better that Eddie had got a boyfriend, they were dating and Eddie had placed a no-sex rule on them for at least two months to make sure that he liked his boyfriend for *him* and not his body. Lewis was flat out amazed at how mature Eddie was being and how much he wanted the two of them to work out.

Yet mostly Lewis was just proud of him.

Lewis held Alex's hand loose as the two of them, Fianna and Ashley went down a long straight staircase down to the reception after another great Mythbusting session. Lewis was pleased with how it went, there weren't many queer people in the class of 60 but he didn't care because today had achieved the session's real purpose.

They had shown all 60 of those straight students that gay people weren't strange, only feminine and they weren't dangers to any of them.

Lewis had loved some of the myths they had busted including a lot about gay relationships, drugs and hook-up culture. They had made some straight students cry about their past and then they had made them cry again later on when they shared inspiring messages for the future.

And Lewis just felt so relieved, alive and happy to be gay as he walked next to his boyfriend after such a great session.

He had noticed a few homophobic students first at all that were giving him daggers at the start of the session but by the end they were hanging onto his every word. Lewis loved that, because he had done his job perfectly.

Lewis thanked the school contact as she opened the door for them all to walk through into the reception area and they all started to sign out.

As he watched perfect Alex sign out, Lewis felt so proud, horny and happy because he was such a lucky guy and it was even better when Alex had done something great for him late last night.

Alex's parents had agreed to loan Lewis the money so he could get private therapy from a therapist that specialised in gay youth suffering the effects of trauma. It would be a long road to recovery and truly accepting him but with Alex at his side he knew he would get there.

Because love really was that powerful.

Lewis and Alex said bye and thank you to Ashley and Fianna, and then Lewis led his boyfriend by the hand through the huge car park filled with endless rows of black, red and blue cars of all different makes and models. And Lewis loved the feeling of Alex's smooth, soft hands in his.

He was beautiful, precious and everything Lewis had ever wanted. And Alex had taught him that no one was going to leave him, he wasn't a bad person and he was just perfect the way he was.

Lewis unlocked his car and kissed Alex's soft, beautiful lips before they both got in and Lewis admired Alex for a few moments. His wonderful hair, his handsome face and his fit as fuck body that Lewis was so looking forward to tasting later on.

"Where do you want to go now?" Lewis asked grinning.

"To the future," Alex said. "The future where

you and me live and love together forever,"

"To the future it is," Lewis said starting the car and as they drove out of the car park he just couldn't stop himself from grinning like a little schoolboy.

This was everything he had ever wanted and he was going to love, treasure and admire Alex forever because he was that perfect.

And as the feeling in the pit of Lewis's stomach relaxed and faded away forever, he was so glad he had met Alex and fallen in love with him. And it had all only happened because he had fallen in love with a Mythbuster.

GET YOUR FREE SHORT STORY NOW!
And get signed up to Connor Whiteley's
newsletter to hear about new gripping books,
offers and exciting projects. (You'll never be
sent spam)

https://www.subscribepage.io/gayromancesig
nup

About the author:

Connor Whiteley is the author of over 60 books in the sci-fi fantasy, nonfiction psychology and books for writer's genre and he is a Human Branding Speaker and Consultant.

He is a passionate warhammer 40,000 reader, psychology student and author.

Who narrates his own audiobooks and he hosts The Psychology World Podcast.

All whilst studying Psychology at the University of Kent, England.

Also, he was a former Explorer Scout where he gave a speech to the Maltese President in August 2018 and he attended Prince Charles' 70th Birthday Party at Buckingham Palace in May 2018.

Plus, he is a self-confessed coffee lover!

Other books by Connor Whiteley:
Bettie English Private Eye Series
A Very Private Woman
The Russian Case
A Very Urgent Matter
A Case Most Personal
Trains, Scots and Private Eyes
The Federation Protects
Cops, Robbers and Private Eyes
Just Ask Bettie English
An Inheritance To Die For
The Death of Graham Adams
Bearing Witness
The Twelve
The Wrong Body
The Assassination Of Bettie English
Wining And Dying
Eight Hours
Uniformed Cabal
A Case Most Christmas

Gay Romance Novellas
Breaking, Nursing, Repairing A Broken Heart
Jacob And Daniel
Fallen For A Lie
Spying And Weddings
Clean Break

Awakening Love
Meeting A Country Man
Loving Prime Minister
Snowed In Love
Never Been Kissed
Love Betrays You
Love And Hurt

Lord of War Origin Trilogy:
Not Scared Of The Dark
Madness
Burn Them All

Way Of The Odyssey
Odyssey of Rebirth
Convergence of Odysseys
Odyssey Of Hope

Lady Tano Fantasy Adventure Stories
Betrayal
Murder
Annihilation

The Fireheart Fantasy Series
Heart of Fire
Heart of Lies
Heart of Prophecy

Heart of Bones
Heart of Fate

City of Assassins (Urban Fantasy)
City of Death
City of Martyrs
City of Pleasure
City of Power

Agents of The Emperor
Return of The Ancient Ones
Vigilance
Angels of Fire
Kingmaker
The Eight
The Lost Generation
Hunt
Emperor's Council
Speaker of Treachery
Birth Of The Empire
Terraforma
Spaceguard

The Rising Augusta Fantasy Adventure Series
Rise To Power
Rising Walls
Rising Force

Rising Realm

Lord Of War Trilogy (Agents of The Emperor)
Not Scared Of The Dark
Madness
Burn It All Down

Miscellaneous:
RETURN
FREEDOM
SALVATION
Reflection of Mount Flame
The Masked One
The Great Deer
English Independence

OTHER SHORT STORIES BY CONNOR WHITELEY

Mystery Short Story Collections
Criminally Good Stories Volume 1: 20
Detective Mystery Short Stories
Criminally Good Stories Volume 2: 20 Private
Investigator Short Stories
Criminally Good Stories Volume 3: 20 Crime
Fiction Short Stories

Criminally Good Stories Volume 4: 20
Science Fiction and Fantasy Mystery Short
Stories
Criminally Good Stories Volume 5: 20
Romantic Suspense Short Stories

Connor Whiteley Starter Collections:
Agents of The Emperor Starter Collection
Bettie English Starter Collection
Matilda Plum Starter Collection
Gay Romance Starter Collection
Way Of The Odyssey Starter Collection
Kendra Detective Fiction Starter Collection

Mystery Short Stories:
Protecting The Woman She Hated
Finding A Royal Friend
Our Woman In Paris
Corrupt Driving
A Prime Assassination
Jubilee Thief
Jubilee, Terror, Celebrations
Negative Jubilation
Ghostly Jubilation
Killing For Womenkind
A Snowy Death
Miracle Of Death

A Spy In Rome

The 12:30 To St Pancreas

A Country In Trouble

A Smokey Way To Go

A Spicy Way To GO

A Marketing Way To Go

A Missing Way To Go

A Showering Way To Go

Poison In The Candy Cane

Kendra Detective Mystery Collection Volume 1

Kendra Detective Mystery Collection Volume 2

Mystery Short Story Collection Volume 1

Mystery Short Story Collection Volume 2

Criminal Performance

Candy Detectives

Key To Birth In The Past

Science Fiction Short Stories:

Their Brave New World

Gummy Bear Detective

The Candy Detective

What Candies Fear

The Blurred Image

Shattered Legions

The First Rememberer

Life of A Rememberer
System of Wonder
Lifesaver
Remarkable Way She Died
The Interrogation of Annabella Stormic
Blade of The Emperor
Arbiter's Truth
Computation of Battle
Old One's Wrath
Puppets and Masters
Ship of Plague
Interrogation
Edge of Failure

Fantasy Short Stories:
City of Snow
City of Light
City of Vengeance
Dragons, Goats and Kingdom
Smog The Pathetic Dragon
Don't Go In The Shed
The Tomato Saver
The Remarkable Way She Died
Dragon Coins
Dragon Tea
Dragon Rider

All books in 'An Introductory Series':
Clinical Psychology and Transgender Clients
Clinical Psychology
Moral Psychology
Myths About Clinical Psychology
401 Statistics Questions For Psychology
Students
Careers In Psychology
Psychology of Suicide
Dementia Psychology
Clinical Psychology Reflections Volume 4
Forensic Psychology of Terrorism And
Hostage-Taking
Forensic Psychology of False Allegations
Year In Psychology
CBT For Anxiety
CBT For Depression
Applied Psychology
BIOLOGICAL PSYCHOLOGY 3RD
EDITION
COGNITIVE PSYCHOLOGY THIRD
EDITION
SOCIAL PSYCHOLOGY- 3RD EDITION
ABNORMAL PSYCHOLOGY 3RD
EDITION
PSYCHOLOGY OF RELATIONSHIPS-
3RD EDITION

A Psychology Student's Guide To University
How Does University Work?
A Student's Guide To University And
Learning
University Mental Health and Mindset

9 781917 181952